THE GREATEST GIFT

This book belongs to:

_____

The Unforgettable Adventures of JUNIOR BEAR

THE GREATEST GIFT

Story
Brad & Jen Klassen

Illustrations
Christopher Barkman

Copyright © 2018 by Brad & Jen Klassen

Cover Illustration Copyright © 2018 Christopher Barkman

Cover design by Christopher Barkman - barkmancreative.com

Editing by Kim Rempel

All rights reserved. This book or any portion thereof may not be reproduced or used in any manner whatsoever without the express written permission of the publisher except for the use of brief quotations in a book review.

Developed in Canada
First Printing, 2018

ISBN 978-1-7751743-0-1

Brad Klassen

5 Spruce Cres.
Steinbach, Manitoba
R5G 0G5

juniorbearbooks.com

This book is dedicated to Jesus. It is His story.
May He get all the glory.

To our four children: Hailey, Addison, Zach, and Makenna, may you always go on an adventure as you learn to listen to your heavenly Father's voice.

Today was the day for the big announcement, and Junior Bear was very excited. His father had gathered all of the animals in the forest together, and everyone was curious about what was going to happen.

Mr. Bear began, "I have decided, that what this forest needs is a grand tree house for all the animals to come and enjoy. Since it will be for all of us, we all need to help build it. I want you to bring all that you can."

Everyone loved the idea of a tree house and began to whisper about it.

Mr. Eagle was the first to speak to the group.

"Since this will be a grand tree house, it must be built in the best tree. I offer mine; it is the biggest and strongest in the forest."

Junior was amazed. He looked up at Mr. Eagle's tall tree. It was a big gift.

Filled with joy, the Beaver family offered their gift.

"We will provide all of the wood for the tree house, and we will even make the furniture."

Junior was shocked by their gift. That would be a lot of wood!

Then the Deer family stepped forward.

"A grand tree house needs beautiful decorations. We will bring the most beautiful flowers from our fields every week so the tree house will always be decorated."

Junior couldn't believe what he was hearing. Three different families had given three large gifts. The animals were in awe, and Mr. Bear was pleased. With all their excitement, they began to collect the supplies, and soon a big pile was formed.

As Junior watched, he heard his father's voice: "Junior, do you see who is over there in the shadows?"

Junior looked. He didn't see anyone at first, but then he saw someone move.

It was Mrs. Possum.

Junior remembered hearing about Mrs. Possum. She was a widow; that meant her husband had passed away and she was all alone. The one thing that Junior knew about Mr. Possum was that he had created all kinds of things out of wood and traded them to the other animals in the forest. Even his dad had traded with Mr. Possum a few times.

As Junior watched Mrs. Possum, he noticed that she was carrying a board with a design on it. He squinted to read it and saw the word "Welcome" carved into it.

Junior watched as Mrs. Possum scurried out of the shadows towards the pile of supplies. She gently added her gift to the pile, scampered back, and disappeared into the forest.

"Do you want to know something, Junior?" Mr. Bear asked as he put his large paw around his son.

"That little piece of wood Mrs. Possum put on the pile is the greatest gift anyone has given for the tree house."

Junior didn't understand. "How could one little piece of wood be a greater gift than the flowers, or the furniture, or the tree?" he asked.

"You see Junior, there are other great trees in the forest, so Mr. Eagle will find a new home. There are more logs for the Beaver family, and the fields will have more flowers for the Deer family. But that piece of wood Mrs. Possum gave was the last piece she had left from what Mr. Possum made. When she goes home she will have nothing else to trade and she will have to discover other ways to find food. That's why it's the greatest gift of them all."

Junior now understood. Mrs. Possum had given everything she had to live on.

The day arrived when the tree house was done. Everyone was excited to see the grand opening. The tree was tall, the woodwork was perfect, and the flowers were beautiful. Junior Bear was amazed by it all, but he mostly wanted to see where his dad had put Mrs. Possum's gift.

As Mr. Bear welcomed them all there, Junior found what he was looking for: Mrs. Possum's sign was at the bottom of the staircase. His dad had placed the greatest gift where everyone who came to enjoy the tree house would have to step on it. They would step on that piece and know that they were "Welcome."

That night, as Junior was being tucked into bed, he looked at his dad.

"Dad, the tree house looks great. I saw what you did with Mrs. Possum's gift and thought it was really nice. It's the perfect spot for it."

"I thought you would like that." Mr. Bear smiled as he gave Junior a hug.

With that he said good night, and Junior went to bed knowing that no matter how big or how small, each gift was important to his father.

Do you know why we love Junior Bear stories?

Because they tell us Bible stories!

Read Mark 12:41-44
and find the true story about a woman who trusted God and gave a great gift.

1. Who or what does each character represent in the Bible story?

- Mr. Bear

- Junior Bear

- Mr. Eagle, the Beavers, the Deer

- Mrs. Possum

- The Treehouse

2. Why does Jesus say the widow's gift is the greatest gift given?

3. What do you think the disciples learned from Jesus in this story?

_____

_____

4. Is it easy or hard to give? Why?

_____

_____

In truth, Jesus loved all the gifts, but He wants us to know that even though a gift may look small, it is important to Jesus.

5. What is something small that you can give to Jesus today?

_____

_____

Prayer:

Dear Jesus, thank You that You see all the gifts we give.

Help us to give all we can, big or small. In Jesus' name. Amen

ADDITIONAL RESOURCES

Find all these and more at:
juniorbearbooks.com/resources

Parenting With Purpose
A Simple Guide to Encourage Parents in everyday life to Connect their Child with Jesus.

The Greatest Gift Resources
Here are more resources you can use to go deeper into the story that inspired The Greatest Gift.

Parenting with Purpose: Family Devotion Schedule
The Devotional Schedule will help you bring the Bible to life in your home with fun and practical ideas.
COMING SOON!

Book 2 In the UAJB : The Promise
COMING SOON!